Ella the Superstar

Written by Ian Whybrow

Illustrated by Sam McCullen

Collins

My baby sister Ella loved books.

Ella read to Dad.
She read, “Wah, wah!”

Ella showed her book to Mum.
Mum said, "Read it to me, Ella."
Ella said, "Num, num!"

Ella read to Grandad.
She read, “GRRR, GRRR.”
“Clever girl!” said Grandad.

One day, we went for a walk in the park.
A lady looked into the pram and said,
"What a sweet little baby!"

Ella said, “I'm a tiger. I will bite your nose!”

"I say!" said the lady, and fainted.

A policeman marched over and looked into the pram.
He said, "What's going on here, then?"

Ella said, “GRRR! I'm a tiger.
I will bite your nose.”

"What a cheek!" said the policeman.
"I'm going to arrest you, baby!"

A man was walking his dog. He said, "You can't arrest a baby!"

The man smiled into the pram.
"Hello, diddums!"

Ella said, “GRRR! GRRR! I'm a tiger.
I will bite your nose!”
“Help!” said the man, and he hid
behind the policeman.

I said, "You're all very silly!
My baby sister's *reading.*"
I showed them the book.

Then Ella read, “Wah, wah.”
She read, “Num, num.”

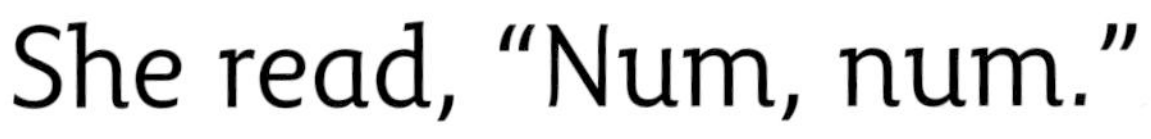

She read, “GRRR, GRRR.”

She read, “I'm a tiger. I will bite your nose!”

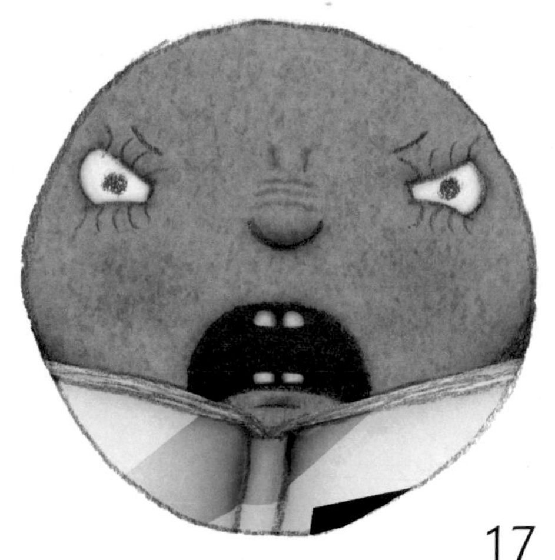

The lady said, “This baby is a SUPERSTAR!
She could be on TV!”

So Ella was the star of her own TV show
and she was in all the newspapers.
She even wrote her own book.

That is how Ella got rich.
Now she can drive a car.
Beep, beep!

BABY 1

Daily News

FULL STORY ON PAGES 2-7

BABY ALMOST ARRESTED FOR READING HER BOOK

Baby Ella reading her book

The policeman who tried to arrest her

TUNE IN TO SEE
Ella
the Superstar
How to be a
Superstar
by Baby Ella
Hear baby Ella
read a gripping tale on TV!
Every Monday, Wednesday and Friday at 6pm on
CHANNEL
24

Ideas for guided reading

Learning objectives: re-tell stories, ordering events using story language; make predictions showing an understanding of events, ideas and characters; use syntax and context when reading for meaning; read and spell phonically decodable two-syllable words; interpret a text by reading aloud with some variety in pace and emphasis.

Curriculum links: Citizenship: Choices; People who help us

High frequency words: a, all, can, dad, day, for, going, her, here, his, in, little, it, me, my, mum, now, of, on, one, said, she, sister, so, that, the, the, to, was, what, will, went

Interest words: superstar, tiger, fainted, policeman, arrest, diddums, gripping

Resources: drawing materials

Getting started

- Look at the front cover together. Read the words and discuss what a superstar is. Can the children think of any superstars that they know (*football players, popstars*)?
- Read the blurb on the back cover. Ask the children to predict what makes Ella a superbaby. Discuss what superbabies might be able to do.
- Look carefully at the picture on the front cover and see if the children notice that Ella is reading. Read the title of the book together.
- Look carefully at the word *superstar*. Using magnetic letters, show children how the words can be broken into two smaller words. Can children think of other words like superstar? (*superwoman, supermarket*). List the children's suggestions on a whiteboard.

Reading and responding

- Read the story together up to p7. Practise using context to establish meaning.
- Reread the story fluently to p7, modelling using different voices to enhance expression. Encourage the children to join in and suggest voices.
- Establish that one of Ella's talents is that she can talk. Ask the children to predict what is going to happen next.